Norman is doomed!

"Elaine's a witch. And she put a spell on me."

"You've been reading too many horror stories," his father said.

"I wish everybody would stop telling me that," Norman complained. "I'm not imagining things. I heard her casting the spell."

"You heard her say, 'Abracadabra, make Norman sick to his stomach'?"

"Not exactly. But I heard her chanting about newts and toads. I don't know what a newt is, but—"

"It's a salamander," his father said. "It's sort of like a little lizard."

"I knew it!" cried Norman. "She's trying to turn me into a lizard!"

NORMAN NEWMAN

My Sister the Witch

NORMAN NEWMAN

My Sister the Witch

ELLEN CONFORD
illustrated by Tim Jacobus

little rainbow®
Troll Associates

Library of Congress Cataloging-in-Publication Data

Conford, Ellen.
My sister the witch / by Ellen Conford; illustrated by Tim Jacobus.
p.   cm.—(Norman Newman)
Summary: Norman is sure that his sister Elaine, an aspiring actress, is really a witch who is casting evil spells on him and his classmate Milo.
ISBN 0-8167-3815-7 (lib.)   ISBN 0-8167-3623-5 (pbk.)
[1. Brothers and sisters—Fiction.   2. Witches—Fiction.
3. Family life—Fiction.   4. Schools—Fiction.]   I. Jacobus, Tim, ill.
II. Title.   III. Series: Conford, Ellen. Norman Newman
PZ7.C7593My   1995   [Fic]—dc20   94-23642

For David . . .
thirty-five years, and still my Teen Angel
—E.C.

To my wife Laura . . .
without her this machine grinds to a halt
—T.J.

CHAPTER

1

"Norman! Time for dinner!"

"Coming," said Norman. But he couldn't lift his eyes from his book. *The Water Witch of Waki-Huna* was the best book he'd ever read. Even better than *The Galloping Ghost of Gopher Gulch*.

Besides, Norman's mother had catered a party the night before. That meant that tonight's dinner would be whatever the people at the party hadn't eaten. And Norman usually found that if party guests didn't want to eat that stuff, neither did he.

"Come on, Norman!" his mother called. "I'm not going to tell you again! And get your sister in here, too."

Norman's eyes raced down the page till he reached the end of the chapter. Clipper, the dolphin mascot of the Waki-Huna Water Festival, was in terrible danger. If Penny didn't get to the festival in time, the Witch of Waki-Huna would—

"NORMAN NEWMAN!"

Norman sighed and reached for his bookmark. The faster he ate dinner, the sooner he could get back to his book. And if he ate *really* fast, maybe he wouldn't taste too much.

The door to his sister Elaine's room was closed. As usual. Norman could hear her voice inside. He pressed his ear to the door.

She was chanting something. Norman couldn't make out the words. They sounded something like, "Double bubble shmubble shovel, I love fruit and toenail glog."

Talking to herself, thought Norman. *Talking crazy to herself. I knew she was nuts.*

He pushed the door open. "Mom says—"

Elaine whirled around. She was dressed all in black. Even her fingernails had black polish on them. All that black made her look pale and thin.

"How many times have I told you to knock before you invade my privacy?" she snarled.

"Two thousand one hundred and sixty-two," Norman answered. "Counting this time."

Elaine's eyes narrowed. "When I am famous,"

she said, "I am going to use all my money and all my power to make your life miserable."

"You don't have to wait till you're famous," said Norman. "You already make my life miserable. Mom says come and eat."

Elaine moaned softly. Their mother's after-party meals were one thing they agreed on. But she followed him anyway.

"It's about time," Mrs. Newman said as they sat down at the kitchen table. "Welcome to our Valentine's Day dinner." She spooned something out of a casserole and passed the plate to Elaine.

Valentine's Day had been two days ago. But the Newmans often celebrated holidays a little late—after Mrs. Newman's customers had their parties and she brought home the leftovers.

Phil the Wonder Dog was sitting under Norman's chair. Norman called him the Wonder Dog because he could do so many neat tricks. He could shake hands, roll over and play dead, sit up and beg, and catch a ball on one bounce—usually.

But sometimes when you asked Phil to shake hands, he rolled over and played dead. Or when you told him to play dead, he sat up and begged.

Elaine made sarcastic remarks about Phil's talent, but Norman knew he was very smart. If Phil didn't do his tricks in exactly the right order, he probably had a good reason.

"It's too bad your father isn't here," Mrs. Newman said. Norman's father was a computer consultant. He had to do a lot of traveling. "I know he's disappointed that he can't celebrate Valentine's Day with us." She passed a plate of food to Norman.

Norman leaned over and sniffed at the stuff on his plate. He jerked his head back and gulped.

"Norman, I wish you wouldn't smell your food before you eat it," his mother said.

"It's too late to smell it after I eat it," he said. "What is this?"

His mother began dishing out the salad.

"Our whole meal has a Valentine's theme. Hearts of palm salad. French-fried artichoke hearts. And this—" she pointed to the casserole dish "—is Texas barbecued beef heart."

"*Beef heart?*" cried Norman. "We're eating the heart of a beef?"

"Don't shriek, Norman. You eat liver, don't you?"

"Not unless you force me." He wished he could go back to his room. No, he wished he could go to Waki-Huna, Hawaii. In fact, he would rather be drowning at the Waki-Huna Water Festival than facing a plate of beef heart.

Norman leaned over and looked under his chair. "You know, Phil looks hungry. Sit up and beg, boy," he urged.

"Don't you dare—" his mother began. But before she could finish the sentence, Phil rolled over on his back and stuck all four legs up in the air.

"What a dumb dog," Elaine muttered.

"Oh, yeah?" said Norman. "I don't see you eating any beef heart."

"I can't," she said coolly. "I'm a vegetarian."

"Oh, sure," Norman said. "Since when?"

"Winona McCall is a vegetarian." Winona McCall was Elaine's favorite actress. Two weeks ago she'd read that Winona McCall only wore black. Elaine had been dressing entirely in black ever since.

"Winona McCall says animals have as much right to live as we do," Elaine went on. "I read the article just this afternoon."

"Good timing," said Norman.

His mother took a forkful of barbecued heart. "It's really delicious," she said. "If you would just try it . . ."

"I wish I could," Elaine said, trying to sound sincere. "I know how hard you work to make— um—interesting meals for us."

Her mother raised one eyebrow. "Elaine," she said, "someday you are going to be a *great* actress."

After a dinner of hearts of palm salad, french-fried artichoke hearts, a peanut butter sandwich, and six heart-shaped cookies, Norman went back to his room.

He picked up his book eagerly and stretched out on his bed. He was on the last chapter when he heard sounds coming from Elaine's room again.

He got up and pressed his ear against the wall. Elaine was repeating those nonsense words. He still couldn't make out what she was saying, but it sounded very mysterious. If she was reading a poem, it was a weird one.

Norman noticed a glass on his desk. He'd had grape juice that afternoon, and he'd never taken the glass back to the kitchen.

In *The Screaming Skull of Saratoga*, Will Marshall had used a glass to listen to the spooky sounds coming from the hotel room next door. In the book the glass worked just like a microphone.

Norman picked up the glass. Which end did

you listen through? he wondered. He couldn't remember how Will had done it.

He pressed the rim of the glass against the wall.

"Umble bumble shmubble . . ."

No help at all. He turned the glass around so that the open end was against his ear.

Now he couldn't hear a thing.

"Darn." It had worked for Will Marshall. Maybe Will had used a special kind of glass.

Norman felt something sticky on his cheek. He rubbed it and looked at his fingers. They were light purple. He looked at the wall. On the spot where he had held the glass, there was a little purple smear.

"Uh-oh." There must have been a drop of grape juice left in the glass.

He licked his fingers and began to rub at the smear. It got larger. The stain didn't look so dark now, but it was spreading like a squashed blueberry.

Norman groaned. "First barbecued beef heart, and now this," he said. "I'm doomed."

CHAPTER

2

Norman walked to school the next morning with his best friend, Milo Burgess. That is, Norman walked. Milo rode in his wheelchair.

Milo had been hit by a car when he was seven years old. He couldn't use his legs, but he was a whiz with his chair. His arms were very strong. Sometimes Norman was gasping for breath by the time they got to school.

"That new Monroe Marlin book was so great," Norman told Milo. "There was this witch who put a curse on a water festival, and every year something horrible happened. Like one year, the star of the water ballet was strangled by seaweed. And this time, Clipper got kidnapped—"

"Who's Clipper?" asked Milo.

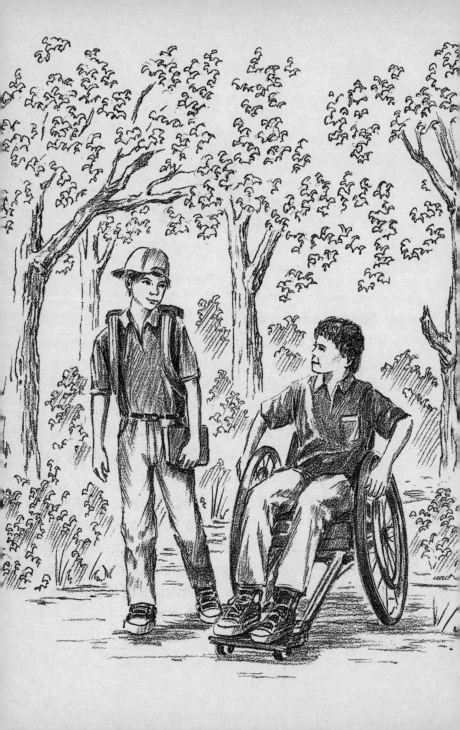

"The mascot of the water festival. He's a dolphin."

"Clipper?" Milo repeated. "A dolphin named *Clipper*? That's not very original."

"But it's a good name for a dolphin," said Norman. "Anyway, forty years ago the witch wanted to be the Water Princess for the festival. Well, she wasn't a witch then, just a girl. And she was a really good swimmer. Plus, she could hold her breath underwater for three minutes."

"Nobody can hold her breath for three minutes," Milo said.

"Will you stop interrupting?" complained Norman. "This is a really good story. Anyway, she didn't get chosen because the mayor's daughter wanted to be the Water Princess, and they picked her instead of the witch, who wasn't a witch before she suffered this huge disappointment."

They reached the school crossing. The guard held up her hand for them to wait.

"Well, she was so mad," Norman went on, "that she wished something awful would happen during the water festival. And the mayor's daughter lost her nose clips right in the middle of the big water ballet and drowned. Ever since then something awful always happens at the water festival."

"Why do they keep having it?" asked Milo. "You'd think they'd catch on after forty years."

Norman scratched his head. "I don't know. I guess it brings in a lot of tourists."

The guard signaled for them to cross. Milo eased down the cut in the sidewalk. "Is that what you did your book report on?" he asked.

Norman froze. "Book report?" he said. "Is that due *today*?" He sprinted after Milo. "Tell me it isn't due today."

Milo shook his head sadly. "It is due today."

Norman groaned. "I'm doomed."

They reached the other side of the street.

"Listen, Milo," Norman began, "could you write a report for me now? Nothing fancy, just a page or two."

"I can't," said Milo. "That's cheating. Besides, what if Mrs. Fergus asks you questions about what you read?"

"You could write it on *The Water Witch of Waki-Huna*," Norman said. "I just told you the whole story. Milo, you have to help me."

"I'll help you," Milo said. "But I won't write it. Hurry up. We only have fifteen minutes."

Norman and Milo raced to the cafeteria. Milo made Norman describe *The Water Witch of Waki-*

Huna again and had him write down everything he said about the book.

Norman wrote so fast that his fingers felt like they'd snap. In ten minutes he had scribbled out a book report.

"See, that wasn't so hard," said Milo as they headed for their classroom.

"Yes, it was," said Norman. "And my hand hurts."

"Your brain's probably sore, too," joked Milo. "It's not used to working so fast."

"Ha-ha," said Norman sourly.

Mrs. Fergus got to the book reports right after the Pledge of Allegiance. "Who wants to share their book with us?" she asked.

Norman kept his eyes on his desk as hands went up around him.

"Lisa, why don't you begin?"

Lisa Cohen read her report about *The Wonderful World of Numbers*. It was very boring.

Norman checked his fingernails. They were clean. He turned his fingers over. There was still a little purple stain on his index finger.

Milo read his report on *The Secret Life of Germs*.

Norman snickered softly. What kind of a secret life did a germ have? All it did was travel around and make people sick. What was so secret about that?

Thinking about getting sick started Norman worrying about lunch. He wondered what his mother had packed for him. What if she'd made him a leftover beef heart sandwich? How would he get anybody to trade?

"Norman Newman."

"Huh?" He looked up, startled. "What?"

"Would you like to share your book report with us?" asked Mrs. Fergus.

"I didn't raise my hand," he said.

Mrs. Fergus frowned. "Didn't you write a book report?"

"Yes," said Norman. "But I didn't raise my hand."

"Well, I'd like to hear it."

Whew! he thought. *It's a good thing Milo made me get this report done!*

Norman walked up to the front of the classroom. He hoped he could read his own handwriting. He'd scribbled so fast that he hadn't had time to be neat.

"*The Water Witch of Waki-Huna*, by—"

"Norman," Mrs. Fergus cut in.

"What?"

"Is this another horror story?"

"It's not really a horror story," he said. "It's a witch story."

"Norman, you've done three book reports this year," Mrs. Fergus began. "They've all been about vampires or ghosts or werewolves. I'm tired of reading about those things."

"I'm not," said Norman.

"Well, you should be. I want you to read something different for a change."

"Like what?" he asked.

"Like anything!" Mrs. Fergus said impatiently. "There are hundreds of books in the library. Read one of them and write another book report."

"Another book report!" Norman cried. "But that's not fair! I just did this one."

Mrs. Fergus looked at his paper. "From the looks of this," she said, "you just did it five minutes ago."

Milo put his hand over his mouth. Norman knew he was trying not to laugh.

"I'll give you the whole week to read another book and write a new book report." Mrs. Fergus looked at him sternly. "Have it in by Friday."

And that was just the first bad thing that happened to Norman that day.

CHAPTER

3

Norman spent the first part of his lunch period scraping the alfalfa sprouts out of his turkey and Swiss cheese sandwich. He spent the rest of the period trying to dry his pants on the hand drier in the boys' room.

Arnold Bean had accidentally-on-purpose knocked Norman's fruit punch into his lap.

He finally got his pants dried. But he spent the rest of the day walking around with a dark red stain on his jeans.

Then he couldn't find his science book.

"It was right here in my desk," he told Mrs. Fergus. "Somebody must have stolen it."

"Why would anyone steal your science book, Norman?"

"I don't know," he said. "But I think you should search everybody in this room."

"I know this is not very likely," said Mrs. Fergus, "but could you have taken it home last Friday? To get a head start on studying for tomorrow's test?"

"*Test?*" Norman gulped. "Tomorrow's *test?*"

Mrs. Fergus sighed. "I knew it wasn't very likely. That's an expensive book, Norman. If you don't find it, you'll have to pay for it."

"Maybe that's the reason it got stolen," Norman said. "If it was expensive, someone could get a lot of money for it. Someone like Arnold B—"

"Norman!" Mrs. Fergus cut him off. "It's *your* book. *You* lost it. Find it."

Norman went home with Milo to study for the science test. But he didn't get much studying done. All he could think about was what a terrible day he'd had.

"And now I'm a stain magnet," he said gloomily. "Grape juice on my wall, fruit punch on my jeans. My mother's going to be really mad. New pants, new paint, new science book. I probably won't get my allowance for the next twenty years."

"How did you get grape juice on the wall?" asked Milo.

Norman explained how he'd tried to spy on Elaine.

"That glass trick doesn't really work," Milo said.

"I found that out," said Norman, "after I got the grape juice on the wall." He sighed. "It's like I'm under a curse or something. All these bad things happening at once."

"Well, we'd better study for the science test," Milo warned him. "Or another bad thing is going to happen to you."

"Even if I do study I'll probably fail," said Norman. "When an evil spell is over you, nothing turns out right."

"Oh, come on, Norman." Milo laughed. "You're not under a spell. You just—"

"That's it!" Norman smacked his forehead. "Ouch." He rubbed his head. "The Evil Elaine put a curse on me! That's why everything is going wrong!"

"Norman—" Milo began.

"That's what she was doing in her room," Norman went on. "That's why she was so mad when I caught her at it. This explains everything!"

"That's crazy," Milo said. "In the first place, there's no such thing as a curse. In the second place, why would Elaine—"

"The *Evil* Elaine," Norman corrected him.

"Okay. Why would the *Evil* Elaine put a spell on you all of a sudden?"

"Because she hates me," Norman said. "And she told me she couldn't wait to get rich and famous so she could spend her whole life making me miserable."

"But she's always hated you," said Milo. "At least, that's what you've said. Why would she only put a spell on you now?"

Norman thought about it for a moment. "Maybe she just learned how. Maybe she always wanted to put a spell on me, but she didn't know how to do it."

"I think Mrs. Fergus is right," said Milo. "Every time you read one of those Monroe Marlin books, your imagination goes berserk."

"It does not!"

"No?" said Milo. "Remember when you read *The Professor from Planet Pylorus*? You thought Mrs. Fergus was a space alien pretending to be a teacher."

"Well, but—"

"And she was going to kidnap all the smart kids," Milo went on, "and take them back to her planet to start a new race of geniuses."

"I wasn't worried for myself," Norman reminded him. "I was afraid she'd kidnap *you*."

"I'm still here," Milo pointed out.

"That doesn't prove anything," Norman said. "Maybe the mother ship just hasn't come back yet."

Milo threw up his hands. "You see?"

"I don't really believe that anymore," said Norman. After reading *The Water Witch of Waki-Huna*, he knew he had a lot more to fear from witchcraft than from spacecraft.

"Here we go again," said Milo. "Norman, forget the Witch of Waki-Huna. We have a test tomorrow. And you have a book report—"

"Book report!" Norman exploded. "Test! How can I think about dumb stuff like that now? I'm in terrible danger!"

Milo sighed. "Yeah. In danger of staying in the fourth grade for the rest of your life."

Norman stared at Milo. "If the Evil Elaine has her way," he said darkly, "there won't be a rest of my life."

CHAPTER

4

When Norman got home, his mother was at her computer in the kitchen.

"Are you working on your cookbook?" he asked.

A lot of his mother's customers asked Mrs. Newman for her recipes. So she'd started to write a cookbook called *Molly's Meals*. Norman was sure no one had asked her for the recipe for Texas barbecued beef heart.

"No," she said. "I'm looking for meatless main dishes." Norman's mother had hundreds of recipes on her computer. "I want to make something for dinner that Elaine will eat now that she's a vegetarian."

"If you don't make barbecued beef heart," said

Norman, "she might not be a vegetarian anymore."

His mother laughed. "You could be right." She pushed her chair back and held out her arms for a hug. "How was school? And what did you do to those jeans?"

Norman hugged her. "Arnold Bean dumped fruit punch on me."

"Why?"

"Because he's a creep. And speaking of creeps," Norman said, trying to sound casual, "where's the Evil Elaine?"

"Still at school," said his mother. "You'd better get out of those pants. I'll see what I can do about that stain."

Elaine was still at school! This was the perfect chance to search her room. Maybe he could find the book of spells she was using.

"There's a purple stain on your wall, too," said his mother.

"There is?" He tried to sound surprised.

"How do you suppose it got there?" she asked. "And don't tell me that Arnold Bean did it."

Norman thought for a moment. "Maybe something purple flew into my room and bumped against the wall."

His mother tilted her head to one side. Norman

could tell she didn't think this was a very good explanation. She made a *tsk* sound and went back to her computer.

Norman headed for his room with Phil at his heels. He changed his jeans and dropped the stained pair on the bathroom floor. His mother was still clicking away on the computer in the kitchen.

"Stay," he whispered to Phil. Then he tiptoed out of the bathroom and into his sister's room.

Phil trotted after him and sat down next to Elaine's bed.

"Yeah, you're right," whispered Norman. "You might see something I'd miss."

He looked around quickly. There were pictures of Winona McCall on all four walls. A poster of a dark, long-haired guy wearing a vest with no shirt hung over Elaine's bed.

The room looked perfectly ordinary.

"Look around, Phil," whispered Norman. "Dogs can sense evil things that humans can't spot."

Phil yawned. He turned around three times and lay down in front of Elaine's desk.

"Of course! The desk!" Norman opened the center drawer. "Keep a sharp lookout," he warned Phil. "She'll kill me if she catches me going through her stuff."

Phil opened one eye. Then he closed it again.

What a mess, Norman thought. Elaine could hide anything in the desk and he'd never find it. He searched through crumpled papers, old tests, Walkman batteries, and little packets of cosmetic samples. Pens, pencils, magazine articles, eight lipsticks.

He opened the next drawer. Rulers, wrist weights, address book, packets of snapshots. Letters, Lifesavers, guitar picks.

Elaine doesn't play the guitar, thought Norman. *Why does she need guitar picks?* It was mysterious. But it didn't mean she was a witch.

In fact, there was nothing in the desk to prove that his sister was a witch. Just a very messy person.

Norman tiptoed over to the bed. He slid his hand under the mattress and poked around.

"Aha!" He felt something. Something smooth and square. He pulled it out.

It was a small white book with a plastic cover. "My Diary" was written on the front. There was a little strap on the edge, with a small gold lock.

"Phil!" Norman said excitedly. "I found something!"

Phil snored softly.

Norman pressed the button on the lock. It didn't open.

"The key," he said. "Where would she hide the key?"

He hoped it wasn't in the desk. He'd never find it in that mess.

He turned toward the closet.

"MONSTER!" came a hideous scream from behind him.

"Ack!" Norman spun around, terrified. The diary flew out of his hand and landed near Phil's nose. Elaine stood frozen in the doorway. But only for a second.

Then she flung herself at Norman, her black fingernails aimed at his throat.

"HELP!" He ducked past her and ran.

"You sneak!" She chased after him. "You worm! You nasty little toad! You read my diary!"

"No, I didn't!" Norman dashed into the kitchen, with Elaine at his heels. "It was locked!"

Mrs. Newman looked up from her computer screen. "Will you two stop screaming?" She rubbed her forehead.

Phil the Wonder Dog padded into the kitchen. He moved between Norman and Elaine and gave one short, sharp bark. Then he stretched, yawned,

and lay down. He didn't like Norman and Elaine to fight. But he was used to it.

"I don't care about your diary," Norman said. "I was looking for—"

He stopped himself just in time. If Elaine knew what he was *really* looking for . . . He shivered.

"Elaine," Mrs. Newman began, "stop this right now."

"Looking for what?" Elaine growled.

"For um—for—" Norman thought frantically. Phil began to scratch his ear. "Flea powder," Norman said.

"Why would I have flea powder in my room?" Elaine asked.

"To get rid of your fleas."

"MOTHER!" Elaine darted for Norman and grabbed his arm. She twisted.

"Ow! Ma, she's breaking my—"

"*That's it!*" Mrs. Newman jumped up and pulled them apart. "Norman, stay out of your sister's room. She's entitled to her privacy."

"I want a padlock on my door," said Elaine.

"And *you*," her mother said, turning to Elaine, "keep your hands to yourself. You're too old for this kind of brawling."

She sat back down at her computer. "Both of

you go to your rooms. Your own rooms. And stay there until I call you. Which may not be till Easter."

"I still want a lock for my door." Elaine stalked out of the kitchen.

Norman rubbed his arm. It really hurt. "Ma, the reason I was—"

"I don't want to hear it, Norman."

"But Elaine's a witch!" he wailed.

"I'm sure she doesn't think very highly of you either. Good-bye. See you at Easter."

Norman trudged down the hall to his room. His arm still hurt. Elaine was so strong. She'd always been able to beat him up.

But now she was more dangerous than ever. Now that she was a witch, she could turn him into a lizard, or make poison ivy grow out of his nose, or even have him attacked by killer seaweed, like the witch of Waki-Huna had done to the water ballerina.

There was no seaweed around the house. But that wouldn't stop the Evil Elaine. She could always have him attacked by killer celery.

He heard her stomping around in her room.

Finally she stopped stomping. For a moment she didn't make any sound at all.

Then she started chanting.

She was so loud, Norman didn't even have to press his ear against the wall. He could hear every word. Every gruesome word.

They sent chills down his spine.

"Eye of newt, and toe of frog, wool of bat, and tongue of dog. Double double, toil and trouble, fire burn and cauldron bubble."

And then she laughed. An evil, terrifying cackle of a laugh.

"Ohhh." Norman squeezed his eyes shut and put his arms over his head.

"I'm *doomed*."

CHAPTER

5

Milo played on a basketball team called the Cyclones. All the kids were in wheelchairs. They had league games every week with other wheelchair teams.

Norman thought the players were amazing. They could do just about everything that an ordinary basketball team could, only they did it zipping around the court in their chairs. When Norman went to the games he got to sit right behind the Cyclones' bench with Milo's father.

Milo was a guard. He wasn't one of the top players, but he was a really good foul shooter. Part of the Cyclones' game plan was to get him fouled as much as possible.

The Cyclone fans cheered whenever someone

crashed into Milo's chair or elbowed him in the head or hit him in the face with the ball.

Milo's father didn't think this was such a terrific game plan. But Norman knew he was proud of Milo—even though he tensed up every time Milo was fouled.

At Thursday's game, Norman was as tense as Mr. Burgess. He had a bad feeling about this game. Of course, he'd had a bad feeling about everything since he'd heard Elaine ranting about newt's eyes and frog's toes.

He didn't know what a newt was, but the whole spell was pretty disgusting.

He'd looked in the dictionary, but there was no such word as "noot." He couldn't figure out any other way to spell it.

"What's a noot?" he'd asked Milo.

"Not much," Milo had answered. "What's noot with you?"

This afternoon, things weren't going well for the Cyclones. Their game plan was working: Milo got fouled three times. But he only managed to sink one of his foul shots.

When the coach called a time-out, Norman leaned over to talk to his friend. "What's the matter?"

"I don't know." Milo shook his head. He looked troubled. "It just doesn't feel right."

Norman got a sudden chill. "*Elaine*," he whispered hoarsely.

"What's your sister got to do with—"

"Yo, Burgess!" the coach barked. "You're not doing that great today. At least participate in the time-outs."

"Coach Perez is really mad," Norman whispered to Milo's father.

Mr. Burgess shrugged. "You can't win them all. And the Hot Wheels are a good team. They took the championship last year."

The ref blew his whistle.

Al Wineberg, the Cyclones' second guard, inbounded the ball to Milo. Milo zoomed down the court toward the basket. He dribbled the ball with one hand, rolling his wheelchair with the other.

"Go, Milo!" Norman yelled. "Take it to the hoop!"

Both Hot Wheels guards charged Milo, one from the side, and one from the front. They waved their arms wildly to block his shot.

One of the guards swatted at the ball, trying to steal it. Milo whirled his chair around to avoid him. Al Wineberg shouted, "Here Milo! Here! I'm open! Pass!"

Milo spotted him, spun around again, and lifted the ball to pass. One of the Hot Wheels tried to block him from the front. The other player shot forward to guard Al.

Milo heaved the ball just as both wheelchairs slammed into his. There was a terrific crash. Milo flew out of his chair and sprawled facedown on the floor.

Norman gasped. He felt as if he'd been punched in the stomach. Kids fell out of their chairs lots of times, but they usually sat right up and were ready to play again.

Milo wasn't moving.

Norman couldn't move, either. The gym exploded with boos and whistles. Milo's father leaped over the Cyclones' bench and ran onto the court with Coach Perez.

Norman clenched his fists till his fingers bit into his palms. He was afraid to look, afraid to see how badly Milo was hurt. But it was even scarier sitting there by himself, not knowing if Milo would ever get up.

Finally he left his seat and pushed through the crowd on the court.

Milo looked horrible. Blood poured out of his nose. His eyes were blank and empty. He was

sitting now, but slumped over, limp as overcooked spaghetti.

Norman squatted down beside him. "Milo, are you okay?"

Milo's head wobbled as he tried to focus on Norman's face.

Norman was terrified. He'd never seen anyone look so bad. "Milo, speak to me!" he begged.

Milo blinked a couple of times. "Did Al make the shot?" he asked.

Norman waited in the hospital emergency room while Milo got x-rayed. The doctors wanted to make sure he didn't have a concussion. It seemed to take forever.

By the time Milo returned, Norman had scared himself nearly crazy. When he saw Mr. Burgess wheeling Milo back to the emergency room, Norman almost threw himself on his friend.

"You took so long!" he cried. "I thought they had to operate! I thought they had to give you blood! I thought—"

"I'm fine," Milo said. "I don't even have a concussion. It was just a nosebleed."

"But you looked so dopey," Norman said as they left the hospital. He climbed into the back of the Burgesses' van with Milo. Now that he knew Milo was all right, he wasn't scared anymore.

Then, suddenly, he felt it again. The bad feeling. The sense that there was something evil hanging over him came back with a *whoosh*.

"Shall we have a little music?" Milo's father asked cheerfully.

"Sure," said Milo. Norman couldn't talk. He could hardly breathe.

Mr. Burgess put on his favorite tape, *Ray Kozlowski's Polka All-Stars*. Milo hooted in protest as his father began to sing along with "Little Brown Jug."

Norman leaned over and grabbed Milo's shoulder. "I knew this was going to happen."

"What?" Milo asked. "That my father would play that stupid tape?"

"No! That something would go wrong at the game. I had this—this *feeling*, right from the beginning. But I just thought you'd lose. I didn't think you'd practically get killed."

"I didn't practically get killed," Milo said.

"It was the Evil Elaine," Norman went on. "She put a spell on you, too."

"Why?" said Milo. "Even if I believed in spells, why would she put one on me? It's you she hates."

"Because you're my friend," answered Norman. "And I'm Elaine's enemy. So anybody who's my friend is her enemy. That's the way the evil mind works."

"Well, I don't know as much about evil minds as you do," said Milo.

"You couldn't," Norman said. "Elaine's not your sister."

"But," Milo began, "if I hated someone so much that I wanted to put a curse on him, I wouldn't just give his friend a nosebleed."

"Hmm." Norman thought about it. "You might be right." He tried to concentrate as Mr. Burgess started to sing "Roll Out the Barrel."

"I've got it! She *meant* to put a curse on *me*."

Milo rolled his eyes. "If you say so."

"But she's new at this witch stuff, right? So her aim was off. The spell bounced off me and hit you instead."

"Norman, that's nutty. Even for you."

"No, it's not!" insisted Norman. "The Water Witch of Waki-Huna put a spell on Hoki-Hoki—"

"Who's Hoki-Hoki?" asked Milo.

"Don't you remember? He was the star clown of the water festival. But nothing happened to him, and Clipper got dolphin-napped instead."

"She did witchcraft for forty years," Milo said sarcastically, "and she still couldn't aim her spells right?"

"That proves it!" said Norman. "Even an expert like the Witch of Waki-Huna can louse up. Elaine's brand-new at witchcraft. Plus, she's not very smart."

"Norman, that was only a book, like *The Professor from Planet Pylorus*. It's not real."

"Maybe the Witch of Waki-Huna isn't real," said Norman, "but the Evil Elaine is. I heard her casting the spell."

"Is that why you got a sixty-eight on the science test Tuesday?" Milo asked. "Because Elaine put a spell on you?"

"Of course."

"Not because you didn't study?"

"How could I study?" Norman asked. "The spell made my science book disappear."

"Okay, okay, I give up," Milo said. "Elaine's a witch, and you're in terrible danger. So what did you read for your book report?"

"Book report?" Norman repeated.

"The one that you had to do over," Milo said. "The one that's due tomorrow."

"Ohh!" groaned Norman, smacking his forehead. "Ow." He rubbed his head. "I completely forgot about it."

Milo snorted. "You're right, Norman. You're in terrible danger. Mrs. Fergus is going to kill you."

CHAPTER

6

Milo stayed home on Friday. The doctor said his parents should keep him quiet for a day or two to make sure he was all right.

Norman walked to school alone. As slowly as he could.

Life was so unfair. Wasn't it bad enough that his sister had put a curse on him? Didn't he have enough problems without Mrs. Fergus on his case?

He got to school just before the bell rang. He walked into his classroom, staring down at the floor. He wished he was invisible.

He slid into his seat next to Lisa Cohen.

"Good morning, boys and girls. My name is Mr. Costello."

Norman's head shot up. A strange man was

standing in front of Mrs. Fergus's desk.

"Mrs. Fergus isn't feeling well today. So I'll be your substitute."

"*Yes!*" Norman nearly knocked his chair over as he leaped up, arms raised.

"Thank you for that warm welcome," said Mr. Costello.

Norman sat down quickly. He hoped the substitute wouldn't tell Mrs. Fergus how happy he was that she was sick.

"This is your lucky day, Norman," Lisa whispered. "You didn't do your book report, did you?"

"Maybe I did, and maybe I didn't," he said mysteriously.

"Right," said Lisa. "And maybe I'm the Queen of England."

It really did seem like his lucky day. Mr. Costello played the guitar, and they spent half the morning learning songs and singing along with him.

In the afternoon they watched a film about growing coffee beans in Africa. It was kind of boring, but there were three good things about it: 1: it wasn't a test, 2: it wasn't homework, and 3: it wasn't math problems.

Then, just before the three o'clock bell rang, Lisa found Norman's science book in her desk. "How did it get here?" she wondered.

"Who cares?" Norman shouted happily. "As long as I don't have to pay for it."

And when he got home, he heard his father's voice in the family room.

"Dad!" He raced into the family room and threw himself at his father. "You weren't supposed to be home till tomorrow!"

Norman's father hugged him. "I'm sorry," he said. "I got finished faster than I expected. Should I go away and come back again tomorrow?"

"No!" Norman laughed. This was definitely a lucky day.

Maybe Elaine's spell had worn off. Or maybe she'd used up so much power with the spell that had bounced off him and zapped Milo, she didn't have any left.

Norman's mother was planning to make Squash Surprise for dinner, but Norman's father insisted that they eat out to celebrate his early homecoming.

"Could we go to Rancho Rick's?" Norman asked.

Norman loved Rancho Rick's. The waiters and

waitresses dressed like cowboys, and there were steer horns and lariats on the walls.

"They only have burgers and barbecue," his mother said. "What will Elaine eat?"

"She could have a salad," Norman said. "And corn and rice. They have lots of side dishes."

"Rancho Rick's it is, pardner," Norman's father agreed.

Norman ordered a deluxe Rancho Rick Range Burger, french fries, cole slaw, and corn on the cob. He ate a piece of his mother's barbecued chicken, and two of his father's Baby Back Ribs Á La Rick.

Elaine had Texas fried chicken and biscuits.

"I thought you'd become a vegetarian," her father said.

"Oh, I did," she said quickly. "But I decided to be just a twice-a-day vegetarian. After all, I'm still growing."

"And Rancho Rick's doesn't make beef heart," Norman added.

She glared at him. "Creep," she snapped.

"Creep-ess," he shot back.

Mr. Newman took Mrs. Newman's hand. He smiled. "It's good to be home," he said.

Norman groaned. "I'm dying." He lay in his

bed, in the dark. His stomach felt like he'd swallowed a volleyball. A volleyball with spikes stuck in it.

Phil put his front paws on Norman's bed and stuck his nose next to Norman's.

"Good dog," Norman said weakly. "Go get Mom."

Phil scrambled onto the bed and walked across Norman's stomach.

"OWWW!"

Phil curled up under his arm and licked his ear.

"I know you want to stay by my side while I'm dying," Norman said. "But you really have to get help."

Phil rested his head on Norman's shoulder.

The door opened. "Norman?" his father whispered. "Did you just yell? What's the matter?"

"My stomach," he moaned. "I think I've been poisoned. Check Elaine's room for a bottle with a skull on it."

"I think you had too much barbecue, pardner," his father said. "Are you going to throw up?"

"I'm going to die," Norman said. "But I might throw up first."

"Let's get you to the bathroom, then."

A few minutes later, Norman staggered out of

the bathroom. His face prickled with cold sweat. His knees wobbled. But at least his stomach didn't feel like it would burst anymore. In fact, it was now empty.

"Feel any better?" his father asked.

"A little," said Norman. "I guess I got rid of all the poison."

"Norman, nobody poisoned you." His father helped him back to his room. "You just ate too much."

"Well, if it wasn't poison, it was the spell," Norman said. "I thought it had worn off. But she must have more power than I realized."

"Who?"

"The Evil Elaine." Norman climbed back into bed. His father pulled the covers up to his chin. Phil jumped onto the bed and walked across Norman's stomach again.

"OWW!"

"What are you talking about, Norman?"

"Elaine's a witch. And she put a spell on me."

"You've been reading too many horror stories," his father said.

"I wish everybody would stop telling me that," Norman complained. "I'm not imagining things. I heard her casting the spell."

"You heard her say, 'Abracadabra, make Norman sick to his stomach'?"

"Not exactly. But I heard her chanting about newts and toads. I don't know what a newt is, but—"

"It's a salamander," his father said. "It's sort of like a little lizard."

"I knew it!" cried Norman. "She's trying to turn me into a lizard!"

"Norman, I know you and Elaine don't get along too well these days, but she cannot turn you into a lizard. Now, I had a long plane ride today, and I'd really like to get back to sleep."

Norman sighed. It was no use. No one believed him.

"Do you think you'll be all right now?" Mr. Newman asked him.

"I hope so," said Norman. "But, Dad?"

"What?"

"If I turn into a newt, will I have to eat bugs?"

"Good night, Norman!"

CHAPTER

7

On Saturday morning Norman went to the library. His stomach was feeling much better. But he knew it was just a matter of time before the Evil Elaine put another spell on him.

He had to find a way to stop her. The library might have a book on how to protect yourself from a witch.

Plus he needed a book for his book report: a short book. With big print.

"Hi, Norman." Mrs. Packer, the children's librarian, smiled at him. Norman put *The Water Witch of Waki-Huna* on the counter under the RETURN BOOKS HERE sign.

"Did you enjoy it?" she asked.

"It was great," he said. "I wish I could read

another one."

"You're in luck," she said. "A brand-new Monroe Marlin book just came in yesterday. I saved it for you." She reached under the counter and pulled out a book. "*Red Fang, Dog of Darkness,*" she said. "It looks pretty gruesome."

"Wow." Norman gazed longingly at the cover. There was a picture of a snarling Irish setter. It had huge, sharp teeth and blood-red eyes. Over the picture was printed: "What happens when a boy's best friend turns into his worst nightmare?"

Norman sighed. "This looks so cool. But my teacher won't let me do any more reports on horror books. She says I have to read something worthwhile."

"When is the report due?" asked Mrs. Packer.

"Yesterday," said Norman.

"So you need something worthwhile and *short*." She grinned.

Norman grinned back. Mrs. Packer was an excellent librarian.

"And I almost forgot," he said. "I need a book about witches and magic spells, too."

"I thought you weren't supposed to read those books anymore."

"This isn't for my report," he said. "I have to—"

He stopped himself. He couldn't tell Mrs. Packer about Elaine. She wouldn't believe him any more than anyone else did.

"All right," she said. "So we need a short, worthwhile book report book. And a nonfiction book about witches."

When Norman got home, he headed for his room. He put the three books he'd checked out of the library on his bed. He knew he should start reading his book-report book, *The Secret Life of Germs*.

But he wasn't really interested in germs. He'd taken the book because: 1: It was short, and 2: Milo had already read it. If Norman didn't get a chance to finish it over the weekend, Milo could tell him enough about it to do a book report.

And *Red Fang, Dog of Darkness* looked so great. The setter with the red eyes and dripping fangs nearly hypnotized him as he stared at the cover.

But Red Fang would have to wait. He reached for *Witches, Wizards, and Magic*. If he didn't learn how to undo Elaine's spell fast, he could be a lizard by lunchtime.

There was no index, so Norman flipped rapidly through the book, looking for key words. Finally, on page 38, he found what he wanted: *Bewitched, Bothered, and Bewildered: Can Witches Really Cast Spells?*

Impatient, he skipped over the first part of the chapter. Of course witches could cast spells. Look at all the bad things that had happened to him since Elaine started chanting about newt's eyes and frog's toes.

The doorbell rang. Norman ignored it, until he heard voices outside his room.

". . . getting so good I scared my sister." It was Deirdre O'Connell, Elaine's best friend.

"Yeah, isn't it gross?" Elaine giggled. "But that's what makes it so powerful."

The door to Elaine's room slammed shut.

Norman's fingers went limp. The book slid out of his hands. A chill started at the back of his neck and tingled down his spine. His whole body broke out in goose bumps.

Deirdre was a witch, too.

And then the chanting began.

Norman listened in horror as Elaine and Deirdre joined in a shrill, evil chorus.

"Double double, toil and trouble, fire burn and cauldron bubble. Cool it with a baboon's blood, then the charm is firm and good!"

They were both casting a spell against him! Elaine had seen that he was okay this morning, so she called her friend for help. Now her evil would be twice as powerful, her magic twice as strong. Between the two of them, they could probably do something even worse than turn him into a lizard.

"Oh, nooo!" Norman moaned. "*Two* witches after me! I'm *double* doomed!"

He grabbed the magic book and ran.

CHAPTER

8

Milo was watching *The Clovis and Cockroach Show* when Mrs. Burgess let Norman in.

"Norman, what's the matter?" she asked. "You look like you've seen a ghost."

"Hey, Norman!" Milo didn't take his eyes from the TV screen. "Come in and watch this with me."

Mrs. Burgess rolled her eyes. "Yes, you watch with him, Norman. I can't stand that junk."

She left the boys alone in the living room. Norman grabbed Milo's arm. "Listen, Milo, you have to help me."

"Wait, wait!" he said. "This is the good part. Look, Cockroach is trapped in—"

"Milo! It's a matter of life and death!" Norman grabbed the handles of Milo's wheelchair. He spun it around so Milo's back was to the TV.

"What are you doing?" Milo said. "I want to watch this."

"Milo, this is urgent. If we don't do something fast, I won't be around to do *anything* with you anymore."

"All right, all right." Milo aimed the remote control backward over his shoulder. The TV clicked off. "What's so urgent?"

"You know Elaine's friend, Deirdre?" Norman began.

Milo nodded.

Norman lowered his voice. "She's a witch, too. And now they're both trying to turn me into a lizard."

"*What?*"

"Or a newt or a salamander or a frog's toe. I don't know what they're going to turn me into. But it isn't going to be pretty."

"You're not pretty now," Milo said.

"This isn't a joke! I heard them." Norman told Milo what the girls had said. He told him about the baboon's blood making the charm firm and good.

"Hmm." Milo bit his lip. He frowned.

"I got this book from the library." Norman handed it to him. "There's a whole chapter on spells. Maybe it'll tell us how to reverse a spell."

"You mean like, 'I'm rubber, you're glue, any spell you put on me should happen to you'?"

"Right," said Norman. "But it's probably not as easy as that."

Milo looked at the book. "Well, I still don't believe Elaine can turn you into a lizard, but it sounds like *she* believes it."

"She doesn't just believe it," Norman said. "She's getting really good at it. She nearly killed me last night."

Norman told him about his stomachache.

"That's bad," said Milo. "The more you believe in her power, the more power she has over you."

"Huh?"

"It says so right here." Milo pointed to the book. "Even if Elaine can't turn you into a lizard, she can make you really nervous. And being really nervous can make you really sick."

"Or dead," said Norman. "Or a lizard."

"Not a lizard," Milo insisted. "So if Elaine believes in spells, she'll believe in reverse spells. If she knows that you're going to fight every spell she casts with a reverse spell, maybe she'll stop trying to put spells on you."

Norman tried to figure that out. "But what if she

can reverse my reverse spells? If you can reverse a spell, can you reverse a reverse spell?"

"Hey, that's too complicated," Milo said. "I haven't even gotten to single reverse spells yet. Wait! Here it is."

Norman leaned over his shoulder. They read the words aloud together.

"One method supposed to combat a spell is to obtain the magic words and recite them backward. This is believed to neutralize the spell's effect."

"What does neutralize mean?" asked Norman.

"I don't know." Milo wheeled to the bookcase and pulled out a dictionary. "But it sounds like what we're looking for."

Norman kept reading as Milo checked the dictionary.

"Of course, to do this, one must know the spell in order to recite it backward exactly."

"I've got it," Milo said. " 'Neutralize: to counter-act the activity or effect of. To make ineffective.' That's it."

"But we have to know the spell," Norman said.

"You heard it."

"Not all of it. And I don't remember it *exactly*."

Milo put the dictionary back on the bookshelf. "Then you have to get it."

"Go into her room again? If she finds out, she'll kill me!"

"But she has to find out," Milo said. "That's the whole point. Your counterspell won't scare her unless she knows you're doing it."

"But if she catches me . . ."

"Look," said Milo. "As long as she thinks she can turn you into a lizard, your life is going to be miserable, right?"

Norman nodded unhappily.

"So we have to convince her that she *can't* turn you into a lizard, or do anything else to you. And the only way to do that is to get a copy of the spell."

"Keep reading," said Norman. "Maybe there's another way to reverse the spell without going into her room."

"But she has to know—"

Norman started to read the next paragraph. "Some believe that a spell can be made harmless by duplicating it. To do this, one must collect the same materials used in casting the original spell."

"Can you do that?" asked Milo.

"Are you kidding?" said Norman. "You think they sell newts' eyes and frogs' toes in Foodtown?"

"Maybe in the seafood department," Milo said.

Norman snapped the book shut. "Not funny, Milo."

"Okay, okay. But I still think you have to get ahold of the spell. And Elaine has to know you have it."

Norman closed his eyes and thought hard. "There might be another way out of this," he said slowly.

"How?" asked Milo.

"Well," said Norman, "I've always wanted to see Alaska."

CHAPTER

9

"Mom, where's Elaine?"

"Hi, Milo," said Mrs. Newman. "How are you feeling?"

"Oh, I'm fine. It was just a bump on the head."

"Where's Elaine?" Norman repeated.

"At the mall with Deirdre. Why?"

"Well . . . uh . . . no reason," Norman stammered.

She eyed him suspiciously.

"I just want to stay out of her way," he added.

"A wise idea," she said. "Look, I have to go out, and your father's working on some reports. Can you boys take care of yourselves for awhile?"

"Sure," said Norman. "Where are you going?"

"I have to see a client about a St. Patrick's Day

party." She gathered up a pile of folders and brochures. "And I have to get the supplies for that anniversary dinner tomorrow. What do you think of green cream puffs?"

"I think I wouldn't eat them," Norman said.

"You're probably right," she agreed. "They don't sound very appealing. Oh well, I'll figure something out."

When she was gone, Norman and Milo headed for Elaine's room.

"See?" Milo said. "This is going to be easier than you thought."

"We haven't found the spell yet," Norman said. "And Elaine could come home any minute."

"If she does, we'll hear her in plenty of time," said Milo. "I'll stand guard while you search the room."

"No, you search," said Norman. "I'll stand guard."

"Why should I do the searching?" asked Milo.

"In case we get caught. She wouldn't beat up a kid in a wheelchair. I don't think."

"We'll both do it," Milo decided. "Two heads are better than one."

"I have no idea where to look," Norman said. He pushed Milo's chair into Elaine's room. "It might be in her diary, but that's locked."

"She was saying it when you left the house this morning, wasn't she?" asked Milo.

Norman nodded. He shivered at the memory.

"And she went to the mall right after that. So maybe she didn't take the time to hide it very carefully." Milo looked around the room. Then he wheeled over to the closet and opened it. "Your sister isn't very neat, is she?"

"You should see her desk drawers," Norman said.

"I will," Milo said. "After we check the closet." He felt in the pockets of Elaine's clothes. Norman shook out all her shoes. Nothing.

"Maybe she took it with her," Norman said.

"Let's not give up yet." Milo wheeled over to Elaine's desk. He reached for the handle of the top drawer. "Whoa!" he said suddenly.

He grabbed a piece of paper that was sticking partway out of a thick book. "I've got it! It's right here, in plain sight!"

Norman rushed to the desk. He grabbed the paper from Milo. "This is it! I can't believe it! How could she leave it just lying around?"

Milo stared at the words. "You know, this sounds like something I've heard before. But I

can't remember what."

"There's no time to think about it now," said Norman. "Let's just copy it before Elaine gets home."

They went back to Norman's room. Writing as fast as he could, Norman started to copy the spell on a piece of notebook paper.

"Boy, this is long," he said. "My hand is getting tired."

"I'll do some," Milo offered. He took the pencil and paper from Norman and began to write. "This sounds so *familiar*. I wish I could remember—"

"Just write!"

When Milo finished, Norman ran to Elaine's room. He stuck the paper between the pages of the large book. Then he raced back to his own room, slammed the door, and let out a deep breath.

"Whew! That was a close call."

"No, it wasn't," said Milo. "We had plenty of—"

They heard the front door open and shut. Then, voices in the kitchen: Elaine and Deirdre.

"Zowie!" said Milo. "It *was* a close call."

"Don't leave me," begged Norman. "Two against one isn't fair."

"All you have to do is say the spell backward," Milo told him. "And make sure Elaine hears you."

"That's the scary part."

They heard the refrigerator door shut, then Elaine and Deirdre's footsteps in the hall.

"Now!" hissed Milo. "I'll say it with you. Do it!"

Norman gulped hard. Voice quaking with fear, he began to recite the spell backward with Milo.

"Good and firm is charm the then. Blood baboon's a with it cool. Bubble cauldron and burn fire, trouble and toil, double double. Wing howlet's and leg lizard's, sting blindworm's and fork adder's. Dog of tongue and bat of wool, frog of toe and newt of eye. Bake and boil cauldron the in, snake fenny a of fillet."

"That'll give her something to think about," Milo whispered

Norman just trembled. He gulped for air like a grounded fish.

They heard a few low words before Elaine's door slammed shut.

". . . don't know . . . don't care . . . my dumb brother."

Norman sank down on his bed. "Do you think she knows what we were doing?"

"She must have recognized the words," Milo said. "She'll figure it out."

"Then she'll know I was in her room."

"If she really thinks she's a witch, you won't have to worry about that," Milo said. "Once she realizes that you reversed the spell, *she'll* be scared of *you*."

"You really think so?" Norman asked hopefully. It was hard for him to imagine Elaine ever being afraid of him.

"I hope so," said Milo. "I never wanted to be best friends with a lizard."

CHAPTER 10

Norman's father was making French toast on Sunday morning when the phone rang. Norman's mother answered it.

"Audrey?" Audrey was Mrs. Newman's assistant. She helped with cooking and serving at parties.

"Oh, no! No, you can't be— Yes, you do sound awful, but— No, of course you shouldn't be handling food, but— All right, I'll manage somehow. Take care of yourself."

She hung up. "Wedding anniversary," she said grimly. "Dinner for twelve. Seven o'clock. And she didn't even make the cake."

Norman's father piled French toast onto a plate and brought it to the table. Phil followed him closely, nose sniffing the air, eyes fixed on the plate.

"We could help," Norman said.

"Sure," his father agreed. "You'll have three assistants instead of only one. You'll get done three times as fast."

"I guess Elaine could help me serve," said Mrs. Newman.

"And she can certainly find something black to wear for a uniform," said Norman's father.

"You're right," said Norman's mother, cheering up. "With all of you helping, I'm sure it will work out just fine."

Elaine got up in a very bad mood. She was grouchy and seemed nervous and distracted.

Maybe the reverse spell is starting to work! Norman thought.

Then again, Elaine was usually in a bad mood, so there was no way of telling if it was the reverse spell, or just Elaine.

She was not very enthusiastic about helping out at the dinner party.

"But I have school tomorrow," she said. "And tomorrow's the—" She interrupted herself. "Winona McCall says that it's *vitally* important for an actress to get enough sleep. Winona McCall sleeps nine hours a night."

"In a coffin, I bet," said Norman.

"Oh, shut up."

"I'll pay you twenty-five dollars for the evening," her mother said. "And you'll probably make another twenty-five with the tip."

"Fifty dollars?" Elaine looked up from her cold French toast.

"And I'll write you a note so you can get to school late," her mother added. "This is an emergency."

Elaine pushed away her plate. "Okay. You've got a deal."

By noon the kitchen looked like a cafeteria hit by a tornado. Elaine stood at one of the double sinks peeling shrimp. Mrs. Newman was heating oil in a large frying pan on the stove. Norman's father was whipping egg whites in a glass bowl.

"I hate peeling shrimp," Elaine grumbled.

"You like to eat them," her mother said.

"What's that got to do with it?" she asked.

"Nothing, really," said Mrs. Newman. "Norman, get the flour and put about two cups in a plastic bag."

She went to the extra refrigerator in the pantry and pulled out two large, foil-wrapped packages.

Norman got the flour canister and a plastic bag. He dumped four scoops of flour into the bag. "What do I do now?"

His mother put the foil packages on the table and opened one. "Put about eight of these in the bag at a time and shake. They have to be coated with flour."

"What are these?" he asked. "Chicken wings?"

"Frog legs," she said.

"*Frog legs?*" he shrieked. "As in, *legs of frogs?*"

"The French love them," his mother said.

"Then let the French coat them with flour," he said. "I don't want to touch them."

"I'll do it," Elaine offered, "if someone else peels this stupid shrimp."

Frog legs, thought Norman. *Yuck.* How could Elaine touch them?

Eye of newt and toe of frog. Toe of frog. Frog legs! And Elaine *wanted* to handle them! Maybe she needed a frog's leg to reverse his reverse spell!

"I'll do it," Norman said quickly. The idea was disgusting, but he had no choice. He didn't want his sister getting her hands on any frog toes.

Pretend they're chicken wings, he told himself as he picked up a handful. "Eww." He shivered with distaste. He couldn't help picturing the frogs these had come from.

"This is so gross," he muttered.

"They taste just like chicken," Mrs. Newman said.

"Then why didn't you make chicken?" he asked.

"Because this is a fancy dinner party," she said, "and chicken isn't fancy enough. Hurry up, Norman. The oil is just the right temperature."

Maybe I can do this with my eyes closed, he thought. He closed his eyes, dumped the frog legs into the bag of flour, and shook.

"Norman, close the bag!" his father said. "You're getting flour all over the place!"

Norman opened his eyes. Phil was shaking himself and sneezing. Flour flew off his fur in great puffs onto the floor, and onto Elaine's black leggings.

"Phil!" she yelled. "No!" She tried to brush the flour off her clothes. Phil rolled over and stuck his paws in the air. Then he wriggled around on his back till his coat was covered with flour again.

"No, Phil!" Norman ordered. "Sit!" Phil stood up on his hind legs and hopped around in a circle.

"Norman, can't you do anything right?" Elaine snapped.

"Not since—" He was about to say, "Not since you put that spell on me." But he stopped himself.

"All right, let's not get hysterical," his mother said. "Cooking can be messy sometimes. We'll clean up later. I've got to get those legs frying."

Norman handed her the plastic bag of floured frog legs. She scooped out a bunch and dropped them into the frying pan. The oil sputtered and crackled. "I think the oil got too hot," Mrs. Newman said.

Suddenly there was a loud popping sound.

"OW!" Elaine jumped back, grabbing her hand. She stepped down hard on Phil's paw. The dog yowled and tried to scramble out of her way.

"Ow, ow, *ow!*" Elaine shrieked.

"Elaine, I'm sorry!" Mrs. Newman grabbed Elaine's arm and stuck it under the faucet, turning on the cold water.

Phil hurled himself at Norman. Norman caught him in his arms and staggered backward into the table. His elbow connected with the flour canister. It flew off the table. Four pounds of flour exploded in a blizzard of white, snowing down on everything in the kitchen.

"Norman!" his father shouted.

Phil twisted out of Norman's arms, hit the floor,

and skidded across the tiles. He scrambled to gain his footing, stumbled, and made a leap for Norman's father.

Phil the Wonder Dog landed against Mr. Newman's chest with a thud. The electric mixer soared across the room. The bowl of egg whites crashed to the floor. So did Norman's father.

Norman stared, horrified, at the scene. His father was sprawled in the middle of a sea of egg-white foam and glittering splinters of glass. The rest of the kitchen was under a layer of flour. Phil was yipping hysterically from another room.

And Elaine kept yelling, "Ow! Ow! I'm *burned!*"

"Keep that under cold water," her mother told her. "It'll be okay. Lenny, are you all right?" She bent over Norman's father.

"Fine," he muttered. "Just dandy. But I don't think we can wait till later to clean up."

Mrs. Newman whirled around and started toward Norman.

"Look what you've done!" she cried.

"Me?" Norman protested. "Did I burn Elaine's hand? Did I step on Phil?" He sniffed. "Do I smell something burning?"

"My legs!" His mother raced back to the stove. She yanked the frying pan off the burner. The oil

spattered, and a tongue of orange-blue flame shot up from the pan.

"Fire!" Elaine screamed. She cupped her hands under the faucet and threw a handful of water at the frying pan.

"No water!" her mother shouted. "It's an oil fire!"

Norman ran to the pantry and grabbed the fire extinguisher. Mrs. Newman had taught them how to use it. He pulled the tab, twisted the nozzle, and aimed it at the stove.

A huge cloud of foam burst from the extinguisher, covering the frying pan, the stovetop, his mother, and Elaine.

"It's out!" he said. "I put the fire out." He waited for someone to praise his quick thinking. But his mother and sister were coughing too hard to congratulate him.

"At least the kitchen didn't burn down," Norman said. Didn't anyone realize that he was practically a hero?

His father looked around at the egg whites, the broken glass, the flour, and the foam.

"It might be easier to clean up if it had," he said.

CHAPTER 11

"There are some things that man was not meant to tamper with," Norman told Milo the next morning.

"That sounds like a line from one of your horror books," said Milo.

"No, I'm talking about real life," Norman said. "I never should have fooled around with a reverse spell."

"It didn't work?" Milo asked.

"Oh, it worked," Norman said. "It worked too well." He described the kitchen disaster.

"So Elaine got a little burn on her hand," he finished. "But my mother lost money on the dinner party because she had to buy all the stuff already prepared at a gourmet deli. And Phil won't come out from under my bed. And my mother blames the whole thing on me."

"That's not fair," said Milo.

"Yes, it is," Norman said. "I didn't actually burn Elaine. But if I hadn't reversed the spell, she wouldn't have gotten burned."

"Ridiculous," said Milo. "It was just a bunch of freak accidents."

"Which I made happen," Norman insisted.

"You did not."

"Well, everyone thinks I did," Norman said. "My mother sent me to my room for life."

"So why aren't you there?" Milo asked.

"I get out to go to school," Norman answered. "What a rotten deal."

At least he'd gotten his book report done. The five hours he'd spent alone in his room hadn't been wasted. He'd read *The Secret Life of Germs,* done a very neatly written book report, and had enough time left before bed to begin reading *Red Fang, Dog of Darkness.*

It was terrific. And very scary.

He'd kept looking under the bed every few pages to make sure Phil wasn't starting to grow fangs.

Nothing awful happened in school, though

Norman kept expecting it to. After all, Elaine had heard him reading the reverse spell. She was sure to be plotting revenge for her injury.

But Mrs. Fergus complimented him for reading a worthwhile book, and Arnold Bean didn't spill anything on him. And when he got home, his mother was waiting for him with a mug of cocoa, a plate of gingerbread, and an apology.

"Norman, it wasn't your fault. It was an accident. If anybody was to blame, it was me. I was under a lot of stress, and I got rushed and careless. I shouldn't have taken it out on you."

She hugged him, holding him close. Norman hugged her back. Her arms wrapped him in a circle of love and warmth. She made him feel so safe that, at least for the moment, he forgot to be afraid of the Evil Elaine.

But not for long.

At four-thirty, the front door burst open. Elaine charged into the house like she was atomic powered.

"Mom! Dad! Norman! Everybody! I made it, I made it!"

Norman peeked around the door of his room. Phil, who had finally come out from under the bed, peeked too.

"She *sounds* happy," Norman whispered to Phil. "She doesn't sound like she wants to kill me."

"What is it?" he heard his mother ask. "I've never seen you so excited."

Norman edged toward the kitchen, in case Elaine's joyous mood was a trick to lure him to his doom.

"I made it! The tryouts were today, and I'm in!"

"In what?" he asked, reaching the kitchen.

She turned to him, beaming with happiness. "The Thackeray Thespians."

"Huh?" Thackeray was the name of her school, but what in the world were thess-pee-ans?

"The drama club, silly. They hardly ever take ninth graders, but they took me!"

"Oh, honey, that's wonderful!" her mother said. "I didn't even know you were trying out."

The phone rang. "Get that, will you, Norman?" Mrs. Newman said.

Norman picked up the phone. "Hello?"

"What did you have to do for the tryouts?" Mrs. Newman asked Elaine.

"I did the three witches scene from *Macbeth*. Deirdre and I did it together. You know, 'Double, double, toil and trouble, fire burn and . . .' "

Norman reeled against the wall. He clutched

the receiver to his chest as Elaine recited the lines that had scared him so badly.

"'Eye of newt and toe of frog, wool of bat and—'"

"It's from a play?" he said.

"Of course, dummy," she said. "Shakespeare. You want to hear my evil cackle?"

A faint voice was piping through the phone. But it was hard to concentrate. Norman's head was spinning.

Elaine wasn't a witch. She'd never put a spell on him. She'd never had magic powers like the Water Witch of Waki-Huna. She'd only been rehearsing a play.

"Norman, are you there?" the phone squawked. "Is *anybody* there?"

Norman put the receiver to his ear. "Yeah," he said weakly.

"It's me," Milo said. "Listen, I finally figured out why that stuff Elaine was saying sounded so familiar."

Elaine was now describing every minute of her audition for the Thackeray Thespians, in between bites of gingerbread.

"It's Shakespeare!" said Milo. "That's where I heard it. It's from a Shakespeare play that has witches in it. It's not a spell at all."

"I know," Norman managed to say.

"You know? Why didn't you tell me?"

"I just found out this minute."

"She wasn't doing witchcraft," Milo said. "She was just acting."

"Probably," Norman admitted.

"Oh, face it, Norman!" Milo said. "You got carried away again, just like you did with *The Professor from Planet Pylorus*."

"Okay, okay," said Norman. Elaine danced out of the kitchen, cackling her evil cackle. "But she's a good actress," he said. "You have to admit she was a very believable witch."

"I never believed it," Milo said.

"You don't know her as well as I do," said Norman.

"Norman! Dinner! Come on!"

"Coming," Norman said. But he didn't take his eyes off the page. *Red Fang, Dog of Darkness* was the scariest book he had ever read.

"Norman, I mean it! I'm not going to call you again!"

"All right, all right!" He sighed and closed the book. He was just at the best part, too. Red Fang had been such a cute little puppy when Timmy got him from the animal shelter. And he was really smart.

The only thing was, sometimes, when he didn't like his food, he got sort of angry. His eyes would turn a peculiar shade of red. His upper lip would curl back, making his teeth look longer and sharper.

As he grew bigger, a lot of the other dogs in the neighborhood turned tail and ran when they saw Red Fang coming down the block.

But the scariest thing was what he did to little Angela's Baby Bootsie doll. . . .

Norman reached down and scratched Phil behind the ears.

"Come on, boy. Let's see what's left over from last night's party. At least we know it's not frog legs."

The dog yawned and looked up.

Norman gulped. Had Phil's eyes always been that way? Why hadn't he noticed before? Could he just be imagining it?

Or were Phil's eyes actually beginning to give off a faint, red glow?

About the Author

Ellen Conford's first book, *Impossible, Possum,* was published in 1971. Since then she has written over thirty books—including *Royal Pain; If This Is Love, I'll Take Spaghetti;* and the *Jenny Archer* series—and become one of the most popular authors for children. Born in New York City, Ellen Conford lives in Long Island, New York, with her husband, David, and enjoys reading, playing Scrabble, doing crossword puzzles, and eating.

NORMAN NEWMAN
and the Werewolf of Walnut Street

by Ellen Conford
illustrated by Tim Jacobus

Norman Newman is back—and his imagination is wilder than ever!

Norman Newman's beloved pet, Phil the Wonder Dog, has a new friend. Everyone thinks Marcel is just an innocent little poodle, but Norman is convinced that Marcel is really a werewolf! Join his outrageous adventures in the next *Norman Newman* book.

0-8167-3719-3 • $2.95 U.S. / $3.95 Can.

Available wherever you buy books.

Look for these other books from

THE BIRTHDAY WISH MYSTERY
by Faye Couch Reeves
illustrated by Marilyn Mets
0-8167-3531-X $2.95 U.S. / $3.95 Can.

MICE TO THE RESCUE!
by Michelle V. Dionetti
illustrated by Carol Newsom
0-8167-3515-8 $2.50 U.S. / $3.50 Can.

THREE DOLLAR MULE
by Clyde Robert Bulla
illustrated by Paul Lantz
0-8167-3598-0 $2.50 U.S. / $3.50 Can.

CAITLIN'S BIG IDEA
by Gloria Skurzynski
illustrated by Cathy Diefendorf
0-8167-3592-1 $2.50 U.S. / $3.50 Can.

THE WORLD'S GREATEST TOE SHOW
by Nancy Lamb and Muff Singer
illustrated by Blanche Sims
0-8167-3323-6 $2.50 U.S. / $3.50 Can.

Available wherever you buy books.